For Tim and Nathalie Bacon

The coastal and interior regions of what is now California were once inhabited by seven distinct groupings of Miwok Indians. This tale is one of the surviving vestiges of an elaborate culture of hunter-gatherers which has virtually vanished. There remain only about 200 Miwok, equally divided between the interior and the coast. For this retelling, the author has drawn on the following sources: *The Folk-Lore Record, Volume V* (London ,1882) and *The Voice of Coyote*, J. Frank Dobie (Little Brown & Co., Boston, 1949).

Lord of the Animals copyright © Frances Lincoln Limited 1997
Text and illustrations copyright © Fiona French 1997

Published in the United States in 1997 by
The Millbrook Press, 2 Old New Milford Road
Brookfield, Connecticut 06804

First published in Great Britain in 1997 by
Frances Lincoln Limited, 4 Torriano Mews
Torriano Avenue, London NW5 2RZ

Printed in Hong Kong

9 8 7 6 5 4 3 2 1

Library of Congress Cataloging–in–Publication Data
French, Fiona.
Lord of the animals : a Miwok Indian creation myth / by Fiona French.
p.   cm
ISBN 0-7613-0112-7
1. Miwok Indians—Folklore.   2. Miwok mythology.
3. Coyote (Legendary character)   4. Creation—Mythology.   I. Title.
E99.M69F76   1997
398.24'52974442'089974—dc20   96-21410
                    CIP

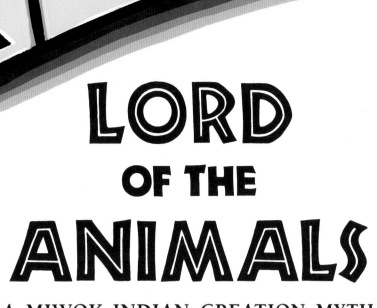

LORD
OF THE
ANIMALS

A MIWOK INDIAN CREATION MYTH

FIONA FRENCH

THE MILLBROOK PRESS   •   BROOKFIELD, CONNECTICUT

Long ago, Coyote created the world and all the creatures in it. Then he sat on the riverbank and gathered a council of animals around him.

"We must decide how to make the Lord of the Animals," he said. "If he is to rule over us, he has to be a very superior creature."

"I agrrree," purred the mountain lion. "The Lord of the Animals must be strong, and he must be swift and silent."

"No, no," said the grizzly bear. "He must have a big growl."

"The Lord of the Animals
must have antlers," said the deer.
"His eyes must see everything and his
ears must hear the lightest
footstep in the grass."

"But antlers would get caught
in the trees," said the sheep. "The Lord
of the Animals must have horns rolled
tightly on each side of his head
so that he can butt hard."

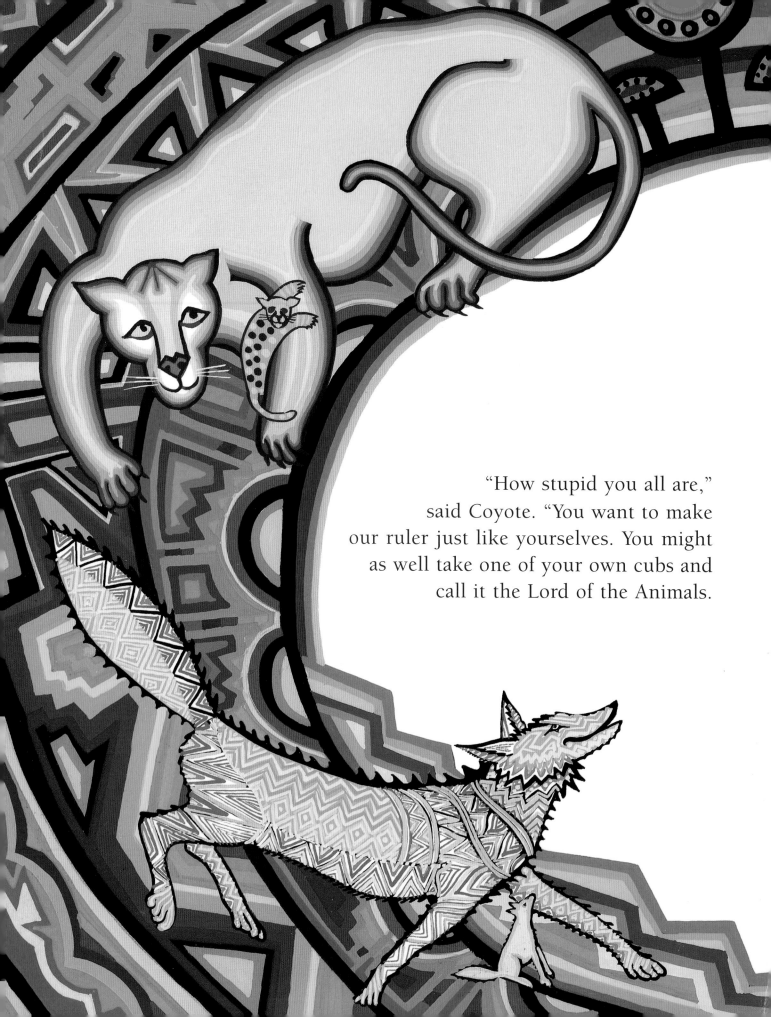

"How stupid you all are," said Coyote. "You want to make our ruler just like yourselves. You might as well take one of your own cubs and call it the Lord of the Animals.

"The Lord of the Animals
should be better than any of us.
His voice should be even more tuneful
than mine. He should run fast and
silently after his prey.

"His feet must be like a bear's, so that he can stand upright. And the deer is right: His eyes must be sharp and his ears must hear the smallest sound so that he can be ready for danger. I don't think he needs a tail. It is a house for fleas.

"And," Coyote said,
    "his skin should be smoother
        than a fish's scales."
    The beaver protested,
        "But without a tail, how will he
            guide himself under water?"

The eagle said, "The Lord of the Animals must have wings to fly above us all."

"And he must burrow deep in the earth," said the mole.

"He must see in the dark," said the owl.

"And what about some nice long whiskers, too?" said the smallest mouse.

"How silly!"
"How stupid!"
Fur and feathers
began to fly.

The owl flew at the beaver,
the mouse bit the lion, and
the bear sat on the mole.

"Stop!" cried Coyote.
"Let us each take
a lump of river mud
and make a model of
the Lord of the Animals.
Then we will choose
the best one."

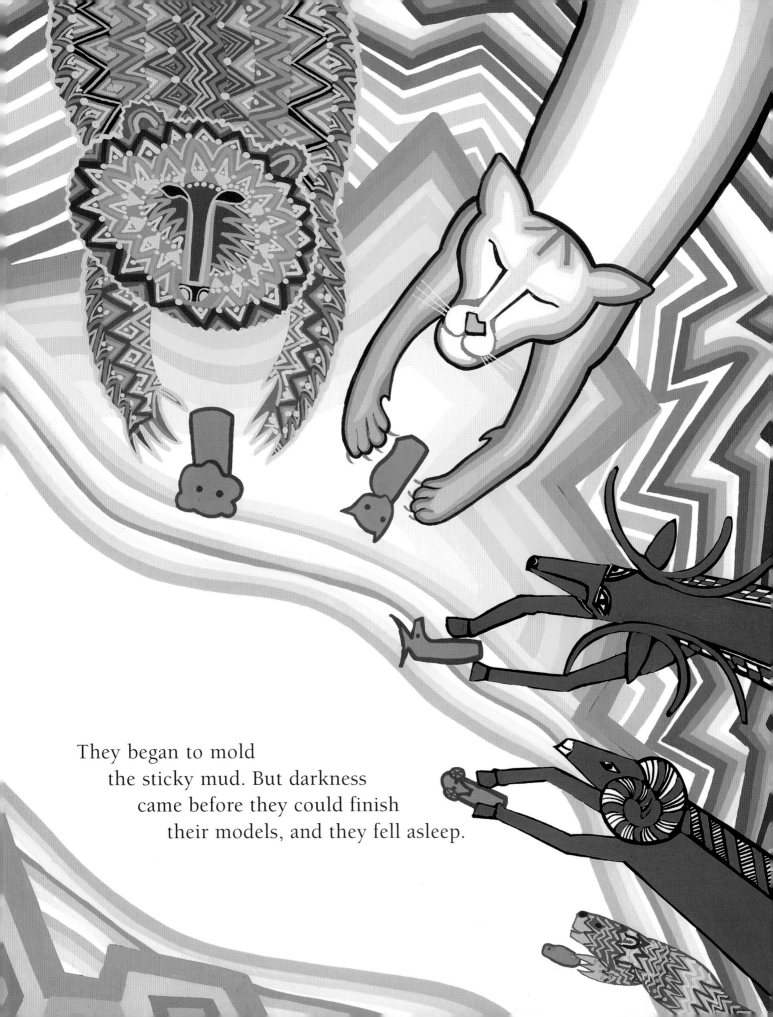

They began to mold
   the sticky mud. But darkness
      came before they could finish
         their models, and they fell asleep.

But crafty Coyote stayed awake all night and made his model by the light of the moon. The river lapped gently over the other models and they disappeared into the water.

In the morning, before the other animals were awake, Coyote finished his model and gave him life.

That is why his eyes can see into the distance and his ears can hear the slightest sound.

Like a bear, he can stand on two legs, and his voice is tuneful.

His skin is smooth and he can swim like a fish in the sea.

But, above all, he is Lord of the Animals because he is cunning and clever—just like Coyote!